Fun at the Beach

by **Damian Harvey** and **Srimalie Bassani**

W
FRANKLIN WATTS
LONDON•SYDNEY

"I want to go to the beach,"
said Dad.

Kenzo did not want to go. "I want to play my game," he said.

"It will be fun at the beach,"
said Mum.

Koko did not want to go.

"I want to read my book,"

she said.

Mum got her hat.

Dad got the ball.

"Come on," they said.

"We are going to the beach."

"It is too wet," said Kenzo.

"It is too windy," said Koko.

"It will be fun," said Dad.

They played with the ball.

"This is fun," said Kenzo.

But the wind

blew the ball away.

Dad ran after the ball.

"The sea is very cold,"

he shouted.

"And very wet," said Kenzo.

The wind blew Mum's hat away.

"Come back," shouted Mum.

She ran after the hat.

"The sea is very cold,"

she shouted.

"And very wet," said Koko.

They made a sandcastle.

"This is fun," said Koko.

The wind blew the bucket away.

It went into the sea

and Dad ran after it.

"I want to go home," said Dad.

"I want to go home, too,"
said Mum.

"It was wet at the beach,"
said Dad.
"It was windy, too," said Mum.

"But it was great fun,"
said Kenzo and Koko.

Story trail

Start at the beginning of the story trail. Ask your child to retell the story in their own words, pointing to each picture in turn to recall the sequence of events.

Start

Independent Reading

This series is designed to provide an opportunity for your child to read on their own. These notes are written for you to help your child choose a book and to read it independently.

In school, your child's teacher will often be using reading books which have been banded to support the process of learning to read. Use the book band colour your child is reading in school to help you make a good choice. *Fun at the Beach* is a good choice for children reading at Blue Band in their classroom to read independently.

The aim of independent reading is to read this book with ease, so that your child enjoys the story and relates it to their own experiences.

About the book

Mum and Dad want to go to the beach. The children don't want to go because of bad weather. In the end it's the children who have all the fun!

Before reading

Help your child to learn how to make good choices by asking: "Why did you choose this book? Why do you think you will enjoy it?" Look at the cover together and ask: "What do you think the story will be about?" Support your child to think of what they already know about the story context. Read the title aloud and ask: "Who is at the beach? What is the weather like there?" Remind your child that they can try to sound out the letters to make a word if they get stuck. Decide together whether your child will read the story independently or read it aloud to you. When books are short, as at Blue Band, your child may wish to do both!

During reading

If reading aloud, support your child if they hesitate or ask for help by telling the word. Remind your child of what they know and what they can do independently.

If reading to themselves, remind your child that they can come and ask for your help if stuck.

After reading

Use the story trail to encourage your child to retell the story in the right sequence, in their own words.

Support comprehension by asking your child to tell you about the story. Help your child think about the messages in the book that go beyond the story and ask: "Why were Kenzo and Koko happy at the end?"

Give your child a chance to respond to the story: "Did you have a favourite part? What do you like to play at the beach?"

Extending learning

In the classroom, your child's teacher may be reinforcing punctuation and how it informs the way we group words in sentences. On a few of the pages, ask your child to find the speech marks that show us where someone is talking and then read it aloud, making it sound like talking. Find the question marks and exclamation marks and ask your child to practise the expression they used for questions and exclamations. The teacher may also be looking at how words can combine to make sentences and joining clauses using 'and'. Go to the example of a joining clause on page 16 and ask your child to point to the joining word.

Franklin Watts
First published in Great Britain in 2017
by The Watts Publishing Group

Copyright © The Watts Publishing Group 2017

Series Editors: Jackie Hamley and Melanie Palmer
Series Advisors: Dr Sue Bodman and Glen Franklin
Series Designer: Peter Scoulding

A CIP catalogue record for this book is
available from the British Library.

ISBN 978 1 4451 5485 5 (hbk)
ISBN 978 1 4451 5486 2 (pbk)
ISBN 978 1 4451 6095 5 (library ebook)

Printed in China

Franklin Watts
An imprint of
Hachette Children's Group
Part of The Watts Publishing Group
Carmelite House
50 Victoria Embankment
London EC4Y 0DZ

An Hachette UK Company
www.hachette.co.uk

www.franklinwatts.co.uk

FSC
www.fsc.org
MIX
Paper from
responsible sources
FSC® C104740